16.99 4/08

W9-BMF-601

NO LONGER THE PROPERTY OF
BALDWIN PUBLIC LIBRARY

What Do We Do with the Baby?

By Rick Walton

Illustrated by Paige Miglio

HarperCollins Publishers

BALDWIN PUBLIC LIBRARY

To baby
Davy Aaron Walton,
our bunny
—R.W.

With love, to Molly Michelle
—P.M.

What do we do
with the bunny?

What do we do
with the baby?

We hold the baby. We hug the baby.

We squeeze the baby.
We kiss the baby.

That's what we do
with the baby.
That's what we do
with the bunny.

How do we move
with the bunny?

How do we move
with the baby?

We rock with the baby.
We bounce with the baby.

We jump with the baby.
We dance with the baby.

That's how we move
with the baby.
That's how we move
with the bunny.

How do we play
with the bunny?

How do we play
with the baby?

We "beep" the nose.
We tickle the toes!

That's how we play
with the baby.
That's how we play
with the bunny.

How do we feed
the bunny?

How do we feed
the baby?

"Open wide!
Choo, choo, choo!"

That's how we feed
the baby.
That's how we feed
the bunny.

How do we clean up
the bunny?

How do we clean up
the baby?

We wash a face,
Some hands,
Some toes.

That's how we clean up
the baby.
That's how we clean up
the bunny.

How do we dress
the bunny?

How do we dress
the baby?

Shirt
And pants

And coat
And hat.

That's how we dress
the baby.
That's how we dress
the bunny.

What do we say to
the bunny?

What do we say
to the baby?

"Peek-a-boo!"
And "I love you!"

That's what we say
to the baby.
That's what we say
to the bunny.

What Do We Do with the Baby?

Text copyright © 2008 by Rick Walton

Illustrations copyright © 2008 by Paige Miglio

Manufactured in China.

All rights reserved. No part of this book may be used or reproduced in any manner whatsoever
without written permission except in the case of brief quotations embodied in critical articles and reviews.
For information address HarperCollins Children's Books, a division of HarperCollins Publishers,
1350 Avenue of the Americas, New York, NY 10019.
www.harpercollinschildrens.com

Library of Congress Cataloging-in-Publication Data
Walton, Rick.
What do we do with the baby? / by Rick Walton ;
illustrated by Paige Miglio.— 1st ed.   p.   cm.
Summary: A bunny mother explores all of the wonderful things she
can do with her baby, from holding and hugging to feeding and dressing.
ISBN-10: 0-06-008419-7 (trade bdg.) — ISBN-13: 978-0-06-008419-6 (trade bdg.)
ISBN-10: 0-06-008420-0 (lib. bdg.) — ISBN-13: 978-0-06-008420-2 (lib. bdg.)
[1. Rabbits—Fiction. 2. Babies—Fiction.] I. Miglio, Paige, ill. II. Title.
PZ7.W1774Wgm 2008   2005020599   [E]—dc22   CIP   AC

Design by Rachel Lynn Schoenberg
1 2 3 4 5 6 7 8 9 10
❖
First Edition